Hound Won't Go

Lisa Rogers
illustrated by **Meg Ishihara**

Albert Whitman & Company
Chicago, Illinois

In loving celebration of Tucker, my sweet, silly,
exceedingly stubborn southern hound—**LR**

To my loving family and friends who inspire me every day,
with more gratitude than I can express—**MI**

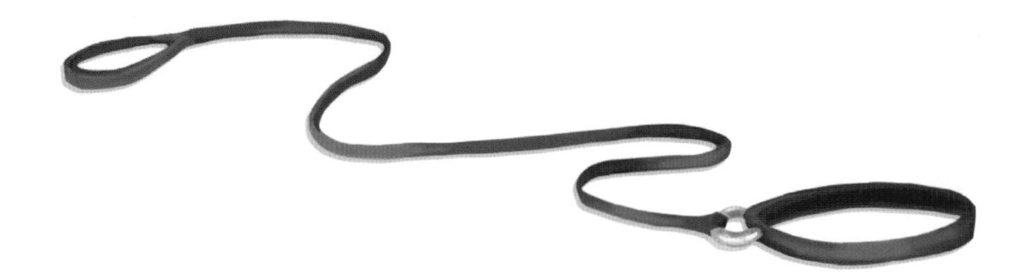

Library of Congress Cataloging-in-Publication data is on file with the publisher.

Illustrations by Meg Ishihara
First published in the United States of America in 2020 by Albert Whitman & Company
ISBN 978-0-8075-3408-3 (hardcover)
ISBN 978-0-8075-3423-6 (ebook)

Printed in China
10 9 8 7 6 5 4 3 2 1 HH 24 23 22 21 20 19

Design by Sarah Richards Taylor

For more information about Albert Whitman & Company,
visit our website at www.albertwhitman.com.

Light flashes.
Hound dashes.

Nosy Hound
sniffs ground.

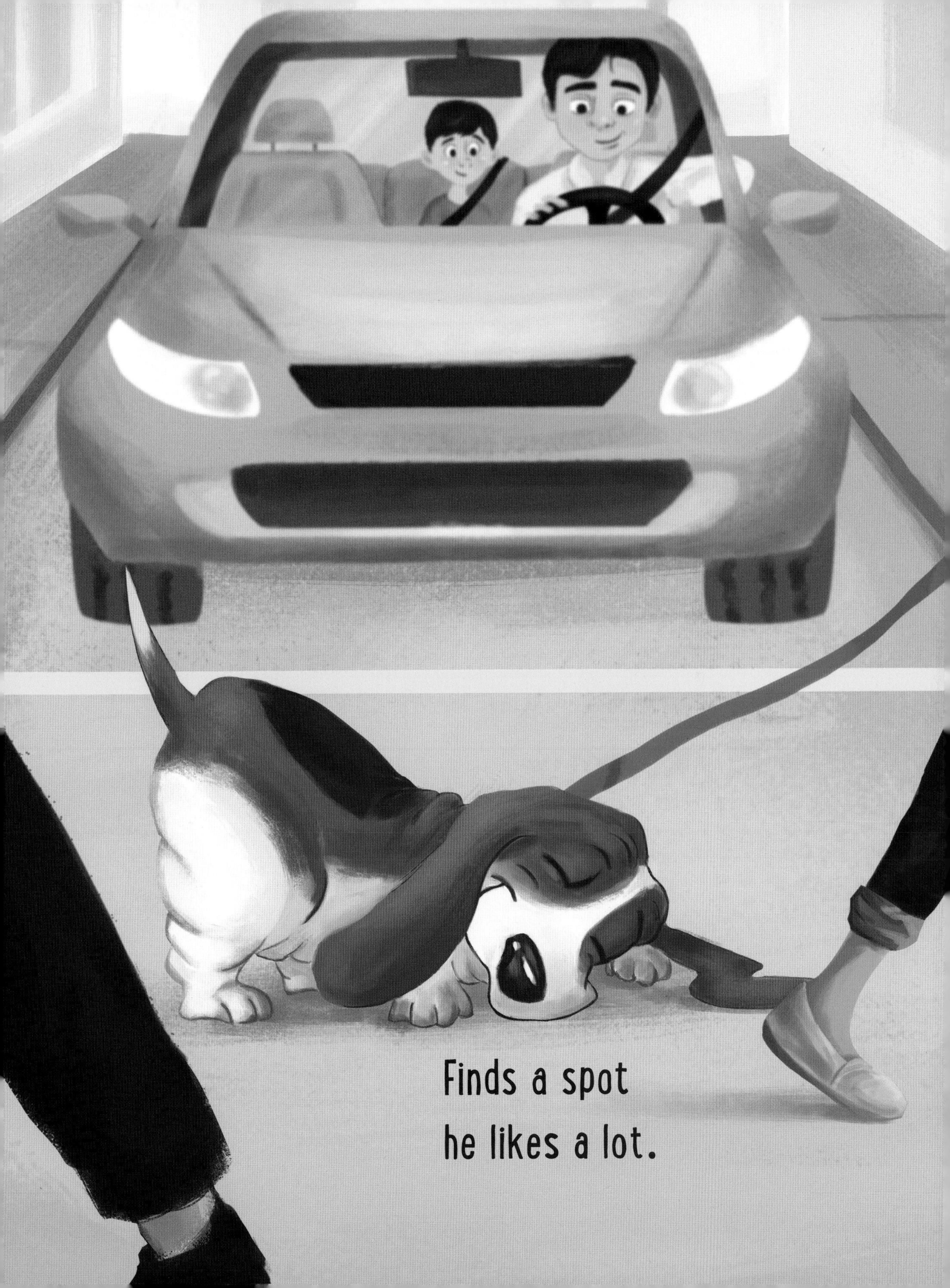

Finds a spot
he likes a lot.

Uh-oh.

Hound won’t go.

Hound stops.
Hound plops.

Light switches.
Hound itches.

Traffic delay—

Hound's in the way.

Time to go.
Hound says no.

Drivers frown.
Hound lies down.

Try a treat?

Hound won't eat.

Tug the rope?
Hound says nope.

People stare.
Horns blare.

Does Hound care?

No.

Hound won't go.

Hound naps.
Then...

Thunder claps.

Whoosh!

Off Hound goes!

Ears flapping.
No more napping.

Splashing feet
pound the street.

Hound goes

and goes

and goes.

Pushes door.
Skids on floor.

Hound drips.

Hound slips.

Shakes awhile.
Makes me smile.

Finds my bed.
Rests his head.

Rain puddles.
Hound cuddles.

Hound, don't go.